MAKE MONEY NOW!™

MONEY-MAKING OPPORTUNITIES FOR TEENS WHO LIKE WORKING WITH KIDS

SUSAN HENNEBERG

New York

Published in 2014 by The Rosen Publishing Group, Inc.
29 East 21st Street, New York, NY 10010

Copyright © 2014 by The Rosen Publishing Group, Inc.

First Edition

All rights reserved. No part of this book may be reproduced in any form without permission in writing from the publisher, except by a reviewer.

Library of Congress Cataloging-in-Publication Data

Henneberg, Susan.
Money-making opportunities for teens who like working with kids/Susan Henneberg.
    p. cm.—(Make money now!)
Includes bibliographical references and index.
ISBN 978-1-4488-9385-0 (library binding)
1. Vocational guidance—Juvenile literature. 2. Teenagers—Employment—Juvenile literature. 3. Money-making projects for children—Juvenile literature. 4. Internship programs—Juvenile literature. I. Title.
HF5381.2.H464 2014
331.7020835—dc23

2012043515

Manufactured in the United States of America

CPSIA Compliance Information: Batch #S13YA: For further information, contact Rosen Publishing, New York, New York, at 1-800-237-9932.

CONTENTS

	INTRODUCTION	4
Chapter 1	WORKING WITH CHILDREN	7
Chapter 2	TRADITIONAL JOBS WORKING WITH CHILDREN	16
Chapter 3	STARTING YOUR OWN BUSINESS	27
Chapter 4	VOLUNTEER AND INTERNSHIP OPPORTUNITIES	38
Chapter 5	WORKING, SAVING, AND SPENDING RESPONSIBLY	45
Chapter 6	THIS IS JUST THE BEGINNING: COLLEGE SUCCESS AND CAREER BUILDING	55
	GLOSSARY	63
	FOR MORE INFORMATION	66
	FOR FURTHER READING	70
	BIBLIOGRAPHY	73
	INDEX	77

INTRODUCTION

The children shriek as the dinosaur piñata explodes. Then they run toward the candy. Eighteen-year-old Andrea Delgado wishes she could stuff a goody bag with candy, too. But she can't. She's in charge. Instead, she chats with the magician. He has made balloon animals for all the children and is getting ready to entertain them with tricks. Parents will soon arrive to pick up their happy children. Another successful birthday party is wrapping up.

Andrea is happy, too. She has been busy all day, checking items off her well-organized list. The birthday boy's mother hired the magician, based on Andrea's recommendation. The teen did everything else. She ordered the cake and bought decorations. She used face paint to transform seven-year-olds into action heroes and organized the games. During the party, several mothers asked Andrea to help them with their children's birthdays.

Andrea loves working with kids. Ever since she was little, she has been organizing the neighborhood children's games and talent shows. Now she wonders how she can fit any more party jobs into her busy schedule. She is proud, though, of her growing bank account. After she pays for her expenses, her net profit for this party will be over $200. Andrea pays for her own clothes and car insurance. College tuition is in the near future. Andrea feels a lot of satisfaction that she is earning her own money. However, she knows that there is more to this experience than just finances. She has learned to think creatively, make decisions, and manage a budget. Andrea has become a businesswoman, an entrepreneur. Like thousands of

A birthday party business is a fun way for teens to make money.

Money-Making Opportunities for Teens Who Like Working with Kids

teens across the country, Andrea has started her own business. In a presentation to a Reno, Nevada, Future Business Leaders of America (FBLA) meeting, she said that planning parties for kids evolved from her popular babysitting business.

You, too, can earn your own income while still in your teens. Opportunities abound for teens who are willing to work hard.

Traditional child-focused jobs such as coaching and babysitting will always need responsible teens who love working with kids. Museums, camps, theme parks, pools, and skating rinks are places where children are the major audience and part-time jobs are generally available.

More adventurous teens might prefer to become entrepreneurs and start their own kid-centered businesses. Teens have successfully taught cooking, Web design, cheerleading, cartooning, and dozens of other skills to children. They have organized themed day camps, babysitting co-ops, and birthday parties.

While earning money is a great goal, many teens have other objectives in working with kids. Some work unpaid internships on the pediatric floors of hospitals. Others volunteer to tutor struggling elementary school students in reading or math. These teens are getting a head start on their future occupations.

Working with kids can be rewarding, lucrative, and, most of all, fun. Whether you work for someone else, or, like Andrea, start your own business, the skills you learn and the money you earn will provide opportunities for your future education and career.

CHAPTER 1
Working with Children

Do you love working with kids? Would you like to translate this love into money-making opportunities? Luckily for you, there will always be jobs for teens who have the patience, energy, and creativity needed to work successfully with children. Parents are busier than ever. They are relying on child-centered businesses to educate, care for, and entertain their children.

You can cash in on these needs of parents to help pay for your needs and wants. And what are these needs and wants? According to a 2008 Simmons Experian survey, teens' top spending priorities are clothing, music, movies, electronics, and video games. Teens are also saving money. College expenses are rising. And many families expect their teens to contribute money toward car insurance and cell phone bills.

BENEFITS OF WORKING WITH KIDS

There are many benefits to working besides the money. Teens learn new skills that will pay off in better jobs and earnings in the future. They gain experience in dealing with stress and conflict. They learn to interact with a variety of people. They gain self-confidence as they take on the adult responsibilities of money management.

Parents and employers benefit as well. Teens generally work for less money than adults. They tend to engage with children easily. Even when they are in positions of authority, teens

Money-Making Opportunities for Teens Who Like Working with Kids

Many teens enjoy teaching skills such as cooking to younger children.

Working with Children

can relate to kids on their level. Some teens are able to teach skills to children that parents may not have time for, such as cooking or crafts.

WORKING FOR OTHERS VS. WORKING FOR YOURSELF

If you'd like to work with kids, you can consider several approaches. First, you need to decide if you want to work for someone else, such as an established business or organization. For example, you might enjoy supervising kids in an after-school program. The advantages to working for someone else include having regular hours and a dependable paycheck. However, there are disadvantages as well. Your job might have little variety and become predictable. Your pay is unlikely to rise much beyond minimum wage.

   Adventurous teens might like starting their own businesses. For example, you might tutor kids in math or teach beginning guitar lessons. The advantage to this approach is that you are in control. You can work as much or as little as you want. You can decide what you want to charge clients for your services. However, there are many challenges to becoming an entrepreneur. You will have to promote your services to recruit clients. There might be slow times when you make little money. There might be stressful times when too many things are happening at once. To be a successful business owner, you need passion, organization, and good money-management skills.

TIPS FOR WORKING WITH KIDS

If you would like to work with kids successfully, what do you need to know? Here are some general tips:

Money-Making Opportunities for Teens Who Like Working with Kids

1. **Get to know the children in your care.** Many children today are used to a lot of attention from their parents. They want to be seen as individuals, not just one of a group. Take the time to ask kids about their interests and talents. Try to find something you have in common, such as owning a pet or playing a sport. They will be a lot more cooperative if they know you care about them.
2. **Establish routines.** Children respond well to predictable routines. Consistent routines help children feel secure because they know what to expect and what is expected of them. Routines also allow activities to run more smoothly and efficiently. For example, create routines for the beginning and ending of an activity. Kids will be more likely to clean up a work area if they know that working together will make it go faster.
3. **Keep directions simple and positive.** Many children have short attention spans. For example, don't say, "Don't run when we are in the hallways." Kids hear the word "run," and that is what they focus on. Also, words like "don't" and "no" can be negative. Instead, state directions positively, such as "Walk inside." Telling children what they *should* do will be more likely to produce the behavior you want.
4. **Avoid power struggles.** When kids argue with you, it is natural to want to argue back. However, this is not productive.

Working with Children

Setting up routines for cleaning up will help children know what is expected of them.

Rather, simply tell the children what you need them to do and what will happen if they don't do it. Then follow through with the consequences. For example, when you ask a child to clean up a work area, he or she might test you by saying, "You are not my parent, and I don't have to do what you say." You might reply, "You're right. I'm not your parent. And we all know that

Money-Making Opportunities for Teens Who Like Working with Kids

Learning about children with disabilities will help you understand their needs.

Working with Children

only when we clean up our table do we get to go outside for games." The child then knows what is expected and what happens if the expected behavior doesn't occur.

5. **Teach children social skills.** Many children are very smart, but they haven't learned how to share, wait their turn, or say "please" and "thank-you." They may form cliques or exclude other kids. Taking the time to demonstrate, practice, and model good social skills will pay off in better behavior. Use every opportunity to show the children in your care the benefits of good manners. Though it may be exhausting initially, kids learn fast. They will soon discover that activities are more fun when everyone acts appropriately.

DISABILITIES YOU MAY ENCOUNTER

You may encounter children with a wide variety of disabilities. Some are obvious, such as children who wear a brace, use a hearing aid, or sit in a wheelchair. Some, such as learning disabilities or mental illness, are less detectable. Here are some of the major disabilities you might find in your work with children:

- **Physical disabilities.** Children may wear a brace or sit in a wheelchair because of accidents or because of defects that happened before or at birth. Some diseases that cause physical disabilities include cerebral palsy, muscular dystrophy, and spina bifida. Visual or hearing impairments can also have multiple causes.
- **Learning disabilities.** Some children have normal intelligence but have difficulty learning to speak, read, write, or do math. For example, dyslexia is a learning disability that can cause difficulty with reading, writing, and spelling.
- **Developmental disabilities.** Down syndrome, infections, and brain injury can all limit a child's ability to learn and function normally. Children with developmental disabilities used to be called "mentally retarded." This term is no longer used.
- **Psychological disabilities or illnesses.** Examples of these include depression, bipolar disorder, anxiety disorders, ADHD, and schizophrenia.

> • **Autism.** Children with autism process information differently than other children. They may have unusual behaviors and interests. They also may have difficulty communicating and interacting socially with other children.
>
> When assisting children with disabilities such as these, take your cues from the teacher or other adult in charge. Treat the children with dignity and respect. Acknowledge their need for acceptance by including them whenever possible. Learn as much about their disabilities as you can. Then relax and have fun with them.

CHILDREN WITH DISABILITIES

Children with disabilities enjoy working and playing with able-bodied children. You will be most effective if you see these children as kids first and disabled second. Learn to refer to them not as "blind" or "deaf," and especially not "retarded." Instead, call them "children with visual impairments," "children with hearing loss," or "children with developmental disabilities." Avoid lumping all children with similar disabilities together. For example, wheelchair-bound children have a variety of personalities, skills, and dreams. Here are some tips for working with children with disabilities:

- Being disabled does not give any child an excuse to be rude or demanding. Expect the same level of good behavior as with other children.
- Sit down or squat when talking to someone in a wheelchair. That way you can make eye contact.
- Make an effort to include the child in group activities. Give him or her jobs such as passing things out.
- Give a disabled child a peer buddy. It will make it easier for the child to make friends.

Working with Children

Children with disabilities love to play games with able-bodied children.

- Be alert for signs that a disabled child is anxious, stressed, or overwhelmed. Then provide a place for a calm time-out.
- Be flexible and try different approaches when giving instructions or teaching a skill. Frequently check that the child understands you. Some disabled children may need more time to process what you say.
- Stay in contact with parents. They are your best source of information about the child.

Everyone benefits when disabled children interact with able-bodied children. The children with disabilities feel accepted and appreciated. Children without disabilities learn that everyone has worth and dignity. An inclusive environment is a win-win for all.

CHAPTER 2
Traditional Jobs Working with Children

Are you ready for the world of work? Have you decided to put your energy and love of kids to work in regular or seasonal employment? The good news is that there are many opportunities for mature teens in child-centered businesses and organizations.

Employers know that children naturally relate to teens. High school students also bring enthusiasm and a sense of fun to the workplace. However, teens' inexperience and limited schedule can sometimes be a disadvantage in a competitive job market. To overcome these issues, teens need to use smart strategies in their job search. Once they find a job, they need to act professionally. They also need to apply effective on-the-job problem-solving strategies to resolve any issues that come up.

FINDING A JOB

It hasn't been that long since you were a kid, right? When looking for a job, think back to the places where you enjoyed spending time when you were younger. These might be the perfect places for you to consider working. Before you begin applying, though, make sure you have all the tools you need to conduct a productive job search. Here are some steps to take:

1. **Prepare a résumé and cover letter.** You can send them to the hiring managers of organizations where you want to work. Or you can attach them to an application for that extra touch of professionalism.

Traditional Jobs Working with Children

Creating an effective résumé is an important step in searching for jobs.

2. **Network.** According to Cornell University Career Services, most jobs are found through networking. This means letting family and friends know that you are looking for a specific type of work. Jobs listed on Web sites are seen by hundreds of thousands of job seekers. You are unlikely to get a response from your application. However, your network of acquaintances might know of an open position before it is advertised.

3. **Check your digital footprint.** A 2012 survey by CareerBuilder.com found that 37 percent of hiring managers check out a potential employee's social media presence on sites such as Twitter and Facebook. They use social media content to evaluate character and personality. Many reported that seeing inappropriate photos on a candidate's profile made them decide not to hire someone. Clean up your pages so that they

Money-Making Opportunities for Teens Who Like Working with Kids

only show you at your best. Write a note on your Facebook wall about your job search. If you are over thirteen, you can also use Twitter to find job possibilities. Sign up to follow companies or organizations where you would like to work. These places might post hints that they are expanding or need more workers.

4. **Be organized and persistent.** Make a list of your preferred workplaces and check with them regularly, such as every few weeks. A preschool that has no openings one week might suddenly have a teaching assistant leave. The hiring director will think of you if you have been calling periodically about open positions.

5. **Be flexible.** Don't be afraid of starting at the bottom or taking a job that is not quite what you want. Though you may want to work in the activity center in the children's museum, a position in the gift shop will get your foot in the door. Then you will be available and familiar to staff when your desired position opens up.

TYPES OF JOBS WITH KIDS

According to the Federal Interagency Forum on Child and Family Statistics, in 2012 children ages seventeen and under made up about 24 percent of the American population. Caring for, educating, and entertaining children have become important parts of our economy. Depending on the size of your community, you can find numerous opportunities to work with children. You can organize your job search by location, age group you'd like to work with, or type of job.

WORKING WITH YOUNG CHILDREN

If you enjoy infants and toddlers, you might target day care centers and preschools. Some of these are franchises of large corporations, and some are small businesses run by local

Traditional Jobs Working with Children

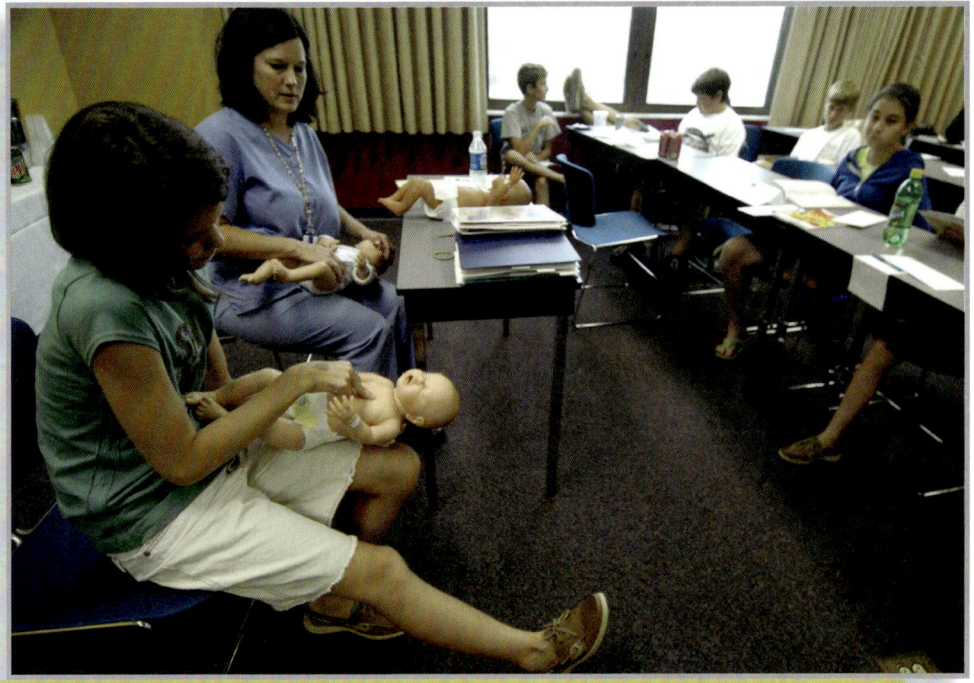

A girl practices clearing the airway of a choking infant during an American Red Cross babysitting course. A class on child care will give you confidence that you can handle emergencies.

entrepreneurs. Others are nonprofits organized by local governments or religious institutions. Most states require day care assistants or teacher's aides to be at least sixteen. Some employers require their workers to take a Red Cross first-aid or cardiopulmonary resuscitation (CPR) course. Many also require employees to get fingerprinted through their local police department. Your work hours would most likely be after school. Most day care centers are not open on weekends.

WORKING WITH SCHOOL-AGE CHILDREN

You may be thinking of a teaching career in the future. If so, you might look into before- and after-school programs at local elementary schools. These programs offer supervision for

Money-Making Opportunities for Teens Who Like Working with Kids

children while parents are at work. Your duties might include preparing snacks, helping with homework, and organizing games or crafts. These kinds of jobs will likely fit well with your school schedule.

Another school-related job is tutoring. A great reference from your English or math teacher might help you get a job with a tutoring business. These for-profit businesses specialize in boosting reading and math test scores. They also help struggling students with spelling, vocabulary, reading comprehension, and math problem solving. Elementary schools or nonprofit organizations such as the Boys & Girls Clubs of America sometimes hire tutors.

There are many places to consider applying for a job if you are athletic. Some of these include gyms, dance studios, skating rinks, bowling alleys, tennis clubs, batting cages, swimming pools, and ski slopes. You might be able to teach lessons at these venues. Or you might supervise open play. Sometimes certifications are needed. For example, lifeguards and swim instructors need to pass a Red Cross lifeguard or water safety instructor course. Gyms, tennis clubs, and ski resorts might prefer teens who have successfully competed at a high level. Many teen athletes enjoy being able to pass on their skills to younger sports enthusiasts.

Other organizations to consider include zoos, museums, and camps. For example, many larger communities have

Traditional Jobs Working with Children

art, history, or science museums. Some might be dedicated children's museums. Other institutions cater to all ages but have a children's section or special activities to engage kids in their exhibits. Teens might find themselves demonstrating electricity, showing off baby animals, or supervising a historical dress-up activity. Day and overnight summer camps often hire teen

Kentucky teen Krista Baker shares her passion for dance with children.

counselors. They usually prefer teens who have had camp experience. Counselors may need to be competent in swimming, backpacking, horseback riding, crafts, or other activities.

Finally, water parks and amusement parks are found in many communities. They rely on teens to cope with the hoards of children who fill them each summer. Patience and the ability to remain calm under pressure are important traits for teens who apply for these jobs.

ISSUES FOR WORKING TEENS

If you have been successful in getting a job, congratulations! Working a paid job will increase your bank account balance. It will also contribute to your maturity and self-confidence. However, you need to consider the trade-offs. You will have less

Teens who love kids and the outdoors might consider a camp counselor job.

Traditional Jobs Working with Children

free time to hang out with friends. How will you feel when they invite you to the movies and you have to work?

Another important issue is school. You may have to let go of sports, theater, or clubs in order to accommodate your work schedule. Your job may also interfere with study time. The money you make to put toward college tuition may not be worth it if you can't keep your grades up.

A job may also conflict with family time. Parents may still expect the same contribution toward household chores. They may also expect you to join them for family events. Think about the effect your job may have on siblings who need you for rides or homework help. You can occasionally ask for days off or trade shifts with coworkers. But you will inevitably have to make difficult choices about going to work when you'd rather do something else.

RÉSUMÉS AND COVER LETTERS

A résumé is a summary of your skills and work experiences. Its purpose is to show potential employers what you can do. Even if you've never had a "real" job, you can list the more informal work you have done for family and friends.

A cover letter, which accompanies the résumé, introduces you as a potential employee. Its purpose is to highlight the particular skills and experiences that qualify you for the job. If you didn't learn how to write a cover letter in school, you can find many models in books or on the Internet.

Some job applicants think filling out an application is enough. However, including a résumé and cover letter with a job application shows professionalism. It will set you apart from other applicants.

SURVIVAL TIPS FOR EVERYDAY CHALLENGES

There are many challenges for teens who work. Some of these include getting to and from your job and figuring out what to wear. Another challenge is maintaining a positive attitude when you are tired or stressed. Here are some survival tips for working teens.

Transportation can be a huge issue for teens who work. If you have a driver's license and own a reliable car, then you are probably fine. However, take transportation into account when accepting a job. A nearby job that pays less might be a better choice than one at a workplace farther away. Take advantage of any carpooling you can do with coworkers. You will need to subtract bus fare, gas money, or money for a parking space from the money you make at your job.

Many teen workers are required to wear a uniform. Even if you don't love it, make an effort to keep it looking neat and clean. Wrinkled or stained clothing sends a message that you don't care about your job. If you have choices about what to wear, take cues from your supervisors about what is appropriate. When working with kids, you want to wear comfortable but professional clothing that allows you to move. Polo shirts are more suitable than T-shirts with slogans or logos. Casual slacks will impress your boss more than jeans with holes. Keeping your hair off your face allows you to look open and friendly. Remember, when you are on the job, you represent your employer. Also, looking professional can help you earn the respect of kids and their parents.

Even more important than your attire is your attitude. Your employer expects you to arrive on time, energized, enthusiastic, and positive. There is no room in the workplace for gossip, drama, or sarcasm. If you have problems or complaints, follow the proper channels to get them resolved quickly. These

Traditional Jobs Working with Children

Patience and a positive attitude will help you relate well to children as well as gain parents' respect.

behaviors will be recognized and rewarded. Your employer will also appreciate professional behavior with regard to cell phone use. While you may be asked to carry a phone for the safety of the children in your charge, be responsible. Save checking your text messages for your breaks.

Most teens realize that they have to start at the bottom when joining the work world. Entry-level positions are a great way to learn how to be an employee. Teens who work hard and maintain a good attitude can quickly move into more responsible positions.

CHAPTER 3

Starting Your Own Business

Have you decided that you'd rather be your own boss than work for someone else? Would you like to try becoming an entrepreneur? Figuring out what kind of business you want to start is the first step. You might want to think about a business that provides a service, such as babysitting or tutoring. The U.S. Small Business Administration (SBA) is a great resource for teen entrepreneurs. Its teen Web site (http://archive.sba.gov/teens) suggests that you consider your interests and strengths when deciding on a business to start.

For example, teen Michael Willis of Austin, Texas, loved football. According to an article in the *Austin Weekly News*, he also wanted to help neighborhood kids stay out of trouble. He started the Chicago Chargers youth football team, which is a nonprofit organization and free for participants. Another teen entrepreneur was fourteen-year-old Robert Nay. He enjoyed game apps on his smartphone. CNN Money reported that he used equipment and resources from the public library to create the game *Bubble Ball*. Today, he owns his own game development company.

Once you have an idea for your business, the next step is to do some research. Is there a need for your service or product? How much competition will you have? How will your business be better than your competitors'? You also need to consider how much time you want to devote to your business. Will it take time each day, or will your involvement be sporadic? What effect will it have on school, friends, and family? Babysitting occasionally for a few families on the weekend is far different from a daily after-school nanny job.

Money-Making Opportunities for Teens Who Like Working with Kids

KID-CENTERED TEEN BUSINESSES

Opportunities for kid-centered businesses are all around you. Today's busy parents are grateful to find teens who can babysit, host a playgroup, or organize a birthday party. Talented teens can give lessons or tutor a difficult subject.

Babysitting is a natural business for teens. Teenagers are generally available after school and in the evenings when parents need them. The Red Cross offers babysitting and first-aid

Running a weekly playgroup can be both personally and financially rewarding.

Starting Your Own Business

classes. Getting certificates in these classes will give you—and parents—confidence that you can handle emergencies. You can ask around at your school for the going rates to charge.

A similar business is a weekly after-school or weekend playgroup. Many parents would love to have a regular time each week to drop their child off for some fun. This is a good business to run with a friend. You need to have a good head for organization. It also takes some investment in supplies. You can organize each week with a theme. Offer games, activities both inside and outside, crafts, and a snack. Of course, speak with your parents to figure out how many children you can accommodate at one time. State regulations vary, but most allow teens to care for children in their homes without licensing and insurance as long as it is less than four hours per day.

A birthday party business might be popular in your community. Many parents would appreciate help thinking of a theme, shopping for supplies, ordering a cake, organizing games, decorating, and cleaning up. You will have to decide if you will charge by the hour or by the size and complexity of the event. Checking with other party organizers will help you price your business right.

Teens skilled in music or a sport might consider giving lessons. According to an article in *USA Today*, eighteen-year-old Eric Cieslewicz set up a Web site promoting his percussion skills. With eight students, he

29

Money-Making Opportunities for Teens Who Like Working with Kids

hoped to make over $400 a week giving drum lessons. Other teens have offered lessons in cheerleading, hip-hop dancing, and guitar. Amiya Alexander of Michigan started her own mobile dance studio when she was ten, according to an article in *Scholastic News*. Her pink bus travels all over Detroit providing affordable dance lessons to budding young dancers.

There are many other lessons teens might consider as a business. Busy parents might love to have their children learn such skills as cooking, sewing, or crochet. Elementary or middle school kids are not too young to learn the basics of jewelry making, bicycle repair, or Web design from a patient teen with solid abilities.

Amiya Alexander began giving hip-hop and tap dancing lessons to children when she was ten.

Starting Your Own Business

Another money-making service is tutoring. Teens with high grades in advanced English, math, foreign language, and many other subjects can find struggling students who could benefit from one-on-one help. Teachers at local elementary and middle schools may be able to provide referrals.

FIRST STEP: THE BUSINESS PLAN

A business plan is like a road map. It is a written plan to help you figure out where you are going in your business and how you will get there. It is also helpful for showing adults that you know what you are doing. A business plan details what services the business will offer and what money and resources it will require.

Some businesses cost very little to run. For example, babysitting requires only transportation to the job, though some babysitters might invest in some games or DVDs. However, tutoring may require educational materials such as workbooks and math manipulatives or even a laptop computer and educational software. Cooking classes may require significant investment in equipment and materials. To estimate the costs of running a business, you will need to distinguish between fixed costs and variable costs. For example, for a cooking instruction business, buying a set of pots and pans is a onetime, fixed cost. Variable costs include buying ingredients for different recipes each week.

The SBA has a sample business plan for a babysitting business you can use as a model. You can view this plan at http://archive.sba.gov/teens/sample_business_plan.html. The plan uses spreadsheets to show all the financial details needed in a business plan. Your plan can be more or less complex, depending on the size of your business.

CREATING YOUR BUSINESS PLAN

Follow these steps to put together a strong business plan. This way, you will have everything you need to start and grow your business.

The first step in creating your business plan is to describe your business idea and your goals. What services will you provide? Also describe your competition. For example, what similar businesses exist in your community? What can you provide that they cannot? If there is a lot of competition, you may have to find a specialty. For example, if there are many people offering birthday parties, you might specialize in popular "princess" parties for little girls.

Pricing your services will take some research. You can use the Internet to see what competitors charge for their services. Or you can call around to various services and ask. You can try to undercut them, or price your services significantly lower than theirs, to steer customers your way. Charging less for a similar service, however, will impact your earnings. Instead, think of ways you can provide extra value. For example, there may be many bright teens available to tutor middle school students in algebra. To beat the competition, you might advertise that you can throw in some standardized test prep for free.

Also describe how you plan to market your business. How will customers find out about your services? One way is to post flyers and hand out business cards. There are resources in most word-processing programs to help you design these promotional items. Post your flyers where potential customers might see them. Many local cafés, gyms, and grocery stores have community bulletin boards. You can also create business cards to hand out to potential clients. You might even create your own Web site.

Keeping good records is very important in a business. The SBA suggests that you begin by creating a start-up budget. This lists the costs of equipment and supplies you need to begin your

Starting Your Own Business

You can create your own business cards to advertise your services.

33

CREATING AN ORIGINAL BRAND

Most successful companies have an instantly recognizable logo—think of Nike, Starbucks, and McDonalds. You, too, can create a simple logo to put on business cards, flyers, and even clothing. Put the logo next to a catchy business name, and you have your brand. For example, for a princess party business, look online for simple clip art of a crown, or draw one yourself. Position it next to a name such as "Fairytale Parties." Print it in a fancy font on iron-on transfer paper from an office supply store. Apply it to a T-shirt, and you have your business attire. You can also buy sheets of business cards and stationery to print.

business, as well as other business-related costs. For example, you might need to buy printer paper and craft supplies, and pay fees for safety classes. You need to think about how you will get this money.

You will also need to create an operating budget. Usually set up as a spreadsheet, an operating budget tracks operating expenses and profits and losses. With a glance at your operating budget, you can determine how much money you are making—or losing—at any given time.

You need to save all the receipts for items you buy for your business. The costs of these items are business expenses. The receipts will be necessary for tax forms.

It is also important to give your customers receipts for their purchases. A simple way to do this is to buy a receipt book from an office supply store. These are duplicate forms. You fill out a receipt for each customer, and keep a copy for your records.

Putting together a business plan may seem complicated and time-consuming. However, the time you spend organizing your business will pay off. Knowing exactly what your goals are and what you need to reach them will save time and money as you grow your business. These organizational skills will also contribute to your success in the future.

PLANNING FOR SAFETY

Safety—both yours and that of the children under your care—should be a primary concern. You should never put yourself in a situation that would make you, your family, or your clients uncomfortable.

There are some things you can do to help ensure your own safety and the safety of the children you work with. If your parent is dropping you off at a child's house, to babysit or give lessons, for example, he or she should come to the door to meet the child's parent the first time.

If you are having a group of children at your home, make sure one of your parents is also at home. That way, you can assure the children's parents that you can handle emergencies.

You need to learn about any health issues the children have. You also need to be able to contact their parents at all times. These tips will help guarantee children's safety:

- Create an information form for each child under your care. Ask if the child has any health issues, such as asthma or migraines.
- Make sure you have several emergency phone numbers to call for each child.
- If you are taking the children anywhere besides your home, you need permission forms signed by their parents.

Being prepared for any emergencies will provide peace of mind for you and for the parents who entrust you with their children.

Money-Making Opportunities for Teens Who Like Working with Kids

Providing emergency contact forms to parents will inspire confidence in your ability to handle emergencies.

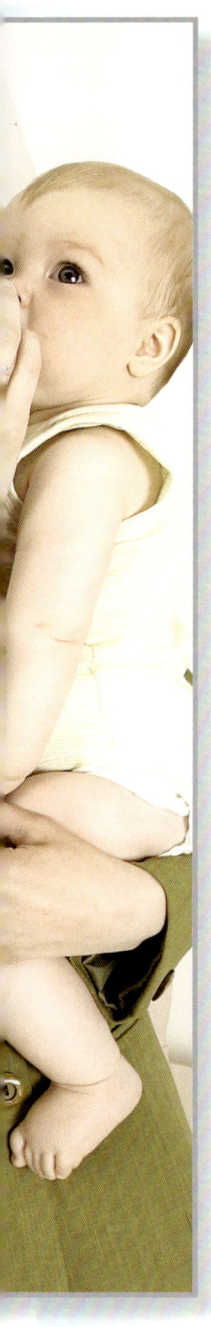

GROWING YOUR BUSINESS

While some small businesses take off immediately, most need constant marketing to grow. You will probably need to advertise to attract new clients. The target audience for your advertising will probably be parents. Your materials have to look professional and be error-free.

Word of mouth is an effective way to get new business. If your clients like your business, they will tell their friends, family, and coworkers. Make sure that you treat your clients politely at all times. Rachel Wood, a teen who cowrote and published her own book on teen entrepreneurship, advises, "If you are competing with other teens, customers will want the most courteous person. Go the extra mile." She also suggests asking clients to evaluate your service. If they like what you have done, ask if they would be willing to act as a reference for future clients. Providing excellent customer service is the key to expanding your business.

Starting a business is not an impossible dream for a teen. Thousands do it every year. With energy, information, and a solid business plan, you can make your dream a reality. You may make a little money for some fun summer activities. Or you may become the next new teen millionaire. Either way, you will come out ahead. You will have learned how to plan and organize, how to manage money and people, and how to create and build something of your own. These skills will provide a foundation for success in the years to come.

Chapter 4
Volunteer and Internship Opportunities

For many teens, volunteer activities and internships are a smart way to explore career interests and gain employment skills. Schools, nonprofit organizations, and hospitals are examples of places where you can work with children. Though you will not make money volunteering, you will be rewarded with the satisfaction of making a difference.

Sometimes an internship or volunteer position can become a paid position. Employers can see what kind of worker you are. If you impress them with your energy, enthusiasm, and willingness to learn, you may be the next one hired.

Your school counseling office or career center is a good place to start if you would like to find an internship or volunteer position. Friends and family members might be good resources as well. You can also go to a particular organization's Web site and search for a volunteer or internship section. Your local librarian can help you identify a number of local organizations to investigate.

Be careful about doing general searches for volunteering or internship possibilities. There are many Web sites that promise placements in different areas of the world. While many of these are legitimate, some are not. Some can be expensive, costing hundreds or thousands of dollars for several weeks in exotic locations. These experiences may be life-changing. Or they may be a pricey vacation with a few "photo ops" with local children. Make sure you check out all organizations thoroughly.

Volunteer and Internship Opportunities

A volunteer position in a school or library can help you learn about a career in education.

39

Money-Making Opportunities for Teens Who Like Working with Kids

TIME MANAGEMENT: JUGGLING SCHOOL AND WORK

Time management can be a huge issue for teens who work. It may seem as if big demands on the job wait specifically for exam time at school. Successful time managers rely on an essential tool—a master calendar. Large wall calendars can help you see the big picture. Planners can be helpful as well. Color-code work schedules, school homework, project due dates, and tests. Also write in family events, social obligations, and extracurricular activities. Jam-packed weeks can be red flags that you are taking on too much. You may have to set priorities and let some things go.

A planner is a great tool for organizing and keeping track of your commitments.

Volunteer and Internship Opportunities

VOLUNTEERING

Many community organizations welcome teens who want to volunteer their time to work with children. There are many advantages to volunteering rather than working in a job or starting a business. Volunteers can often choose their own hours to work. This is useful for busy students who have a difficult class load or a lot of extracurricular activities. Volunteers can also get fun and exciting positions. Many nonprofit organizations cannot afford to hire a lot of people. They rely on volunteers to take on necessary jobs. For example, teens ages thirteen to fifteen can volunteer at the National Zoo in Washington, D.C. They assist with the Summer Safari day camps, teaching children how to interact with the animals. Teen volunteers at the University of Texas M. D. Anderson Cancer Center take craft activities to the children's wards. And the Emergency Housing Consortium of San Jose, California, recruits teen volunteers to help the homeless as "child care champions."

Many large organizations, such as hospitals, school districts, and museums, have coordinators who place volunteers. Teens might entertain children receiving treatments in pediatric wards of hospitals. They might coach disadvantaged children on a sports team. A camp for disabled children might need volunteer counselors to organize games and activities. Or teens might help second graders work on math puzzles in a nearby elementary school. Supervising experiments at a local museum or reading to children at a library story hour are other volunteer possibilities.

There are numerous rewards for volunteering. Leadership, problem solving, and interacting with diverse populations are just some of the skills teens learn in volunteer positions. They gain maturity and the confidence to cope with new situations. Volunteering is also a great way to learn about potential careers.

Money-Making Opportunities for Teens Who Like Working with Kids

Debby Ryan, the star of Disney Channel's *Jessie*, says that volunteering is a cool thing for teens to do. "Discover what you care about, and look for opportunities in your neighborhood to get involved," she told *USA Weekend*. Disney's Friends for Change program encourages teens to become leaders and be a catalyst for change in their own communities.

INTERNSHIPS

An internship is a formal program in which students gain experience in a workplace. It lasts for a short period of time. It is most often unpaid. Teens who work in an internship learn what it is like to be an employee. They usually receive a mentor who helps them gain knowledge about the workplace. The interns learn what habits and attitudes employers expect from their employees. They are able to make connections between what they are learning in school and the skills needed on the job. This can lead to more motivation and higher grades. Often interns can receive high school elective credit, and internships are impressive on résumés and college applications.

Internships are a good way to build skills and learn about careers. For example, before you decide that a career teaching kindergarten is for you, you might want to spend a few weeks or months interning in a local classroom. You might find that while you love teaching, older kids are more your style.

Your school counseling office or career center is a good first stop to find out about internships. Many high schools will arrange internships for students. These can last from a week to an entire year. Friends and relatives can also suggest internship possibilities. Books about internships offer ideas and listings, too.

Volunteer and Internship Opportunities

Consider opportunities that might help you figure out your interests and strengths. Interning with child and youth services in the military might bring out your desire to serve the nation. An internship working with kids at a community arts agency could show your creative side. In any setting, interns learn the importance of good communication and organizational skills.

An internship can give you valuable insights into a potential career.

They learn how to act professionally, maintain a positive attitude, and cope with challenges in the workplace.

Angie Fogle, a New York City fashion intern, thought her internship was very valuable. In a 2010 *Teen Vogue* blog, she said, "It has taught me the importance of teamwork, deadlines, multitasking, and putting forth your best effort, no matter how small or large the task." These skills directly connected with her studies in school.

During challenging economic times, it is sometimes difficult for teens to find a job or start a business. If this is the case for you, consider volunteering or interning. Time spent improving the lives of others and increasing your own employability will pay off in your future. You could find the passion that will drive your life for many years.

CHAPTER 5
Working, Saving, and Spending Responsibly

Whether working for themselves or for someone else, most teens are excited to be earning money. They feel very adult when buying their own clothes and electronics. They are proud to be saving for a big-ticket item such as a car or a college education. Along with these new privileges, teens also take on the responsibilities of working. These include paying attention to U.S. Department of Labor laws and safety regulations. They also include working ethically and paying taxes. Teens need to learn how to set financial goals, use banking services, and use credit and debit cards responsibly. These practices lay the foundation for building a solid financial future.

SETTING FINANCIAL GOALS

You wouldn't start a race without knowing where the finish line was, would you? That's what it's like to save money without goals. You will be tempted to spend your money without thinking about it. Typical places where money just seems to disappear are fast-food restaurants, makeup counters, vending machines, and video game stores.

Take charge of your money by setting specific short- and long-term goals. Review them frequently so that they are always on your mind. Put a brightly colored list of your goals in your wallet or purse. That way, when you take out your money to buy something, you will be reminded that you are saving for your goals.

Money-Making Opportunities for Teens Who Like Working with Kids

It's important to learn to manage money and spend it responsibly.

A good way to think about financial goals is to distinguish between wants and needs. Your wants are the latest gadgets, fashion accessories, movies, music, and video games. Wants might even include high-cost items such as a senior trip or a new snowboard. These items are fun to have. There is nothing wrong with setting aside a certain amount of your earnings to

Working, Saving, and Spending Responsibly

buy these things. You might allot a certain percentage of your paycheck or profits to these wants. However, you need to make sure you can pay for your needs.

Your needs are priority items such as college tuition or car payments. You may also need to contribute toward family expenses. Saving money takes commitment, discipline, and the ability to delay gratification. When your friends are planning a day of shopping, eating out, and seeing a movie, you will have to be strong when deciding to save that money instead. Constantly reminding yourself about your long-term goals will pay off in your growing savings account.

You need to be very specific about the money required to meet your needs. For example, you may decide you want to attend a nearby state college. According to research conducted in 2011 by the College Board, the average price of one year's tuition at a state college is $8,240. Your parents may expect you to pay half that amount, or $4,120. If so, you would need to save about $344 each month for a year to meet the goal of attending college. You might also be saving for a car. Depending on the car you choose (such as new or used) and your loan interest rate, monthly payments for a car can vary by hundreds of dollars. However, a large down payment can lower monthly costs significantly. You also need to consider state registration fees and the cost of car insurance.

For many teens, an important goal is to contribute money to charity. Leanna Archer started her own hair products company when she was eleven. Leanna told *USA Today* that she puts half the earnings from her business into a college savings account. She puts another quarter back into the business. The last 25 percent is donated to a Haitian charity for earthquake relief. Some teens even start their own charities. CNN Money profiled Asya Gonzalez, who at thirteen began her own T-shirt company. She donates a portion of every shirt sold to She's Worth It!, a non-profit organization she founded. The organization is dedicated to ending human trafficking and child sex slavery.

BANKING

In a 2010 Capital One survey, 45 percent of graduating high school seniors said they were unsure or unprepared to manage their own banking and personal finances. That doesn't have to be you. An important first step in becoming financially responsible is setting up checking and savings accounts at a bank near your home.

A checking account allows you to deposit money and then pay bills with paper checks or online. When you are working, it's a good idea to have your employer deposit your paycheck directly into your checking account. This is known as direct deposit. With this method, your paycheck is sent to your bank instead of handed or mailed to you. You get to skip the step of depositing your check, and your funds are available quickly.

Teens under eighteen will need a parent or guardian to cosign a checking account. This means that your parent will have access to the account. Also keep in mind that the bank may charge fees for its checking account services.

In addition to writing checks and paying bills online, you will likely want to withdraw cash using your bank's

Working, Saving, and Spending Responsibly

automated teller machine (ATM). You will pay a fee to withdraw money from other banks' ATMs, so be sure you always use your bank's machines. Also, many accounts allow you to use your ATM/debit card to pay for items in a store. When you use the card, the money is immediately withdrawn from your checking account.

Accurate record keeping is essential to make sure you have enough money to cover payments and withdrawals. It's important to keep track of all your deposits and withdrawals. You also

Teens who earn money need to learn about banking services. If you are under eighteen, your parents can help you open an account.

need to record every check you write and purchase you make with your debit card. The bank will give you a check register to carry around with you. At the end of each month, you will receive a statement that lists all of your deposits, checks, debit card payments, and ATM withdrawals. Learning how to reconcile your checking account, which involves checking your own records against the bank's statements, is an important financial skill. A bank representative can show you how to do this. Today, many bank customers also keep track of their money online, rather than waiting for the bank to send monthly statements.

Keep in mind that if you spend more than you have in your checking account, your account will be overdrawn. Banks charge fees for this, and they can cost you a lot of money. Eighteen-year-old Erin Walker opened her first bank account with a large national bank in California. According to an article in *Consumer Reports*, she was charged $506 in fees for an overdraft of about $120. Banks typically charge $30 to $35 each time an overdraft occurs. They do this even for very small purchases that send your account into negative territory, such as a $4 drink at Jamba Juice. That is why you need to keep close track of your checking account balance.

While a checking account gives you fast access to your money, it typically does not pay interest. You may also want to open a savings account. Almost all savings accounts pay interest. Each month, the bank calculates the interest and provides a statement. Interest rates on savings accounts have been low in recent years. However, the money is safe and out of danger of being spent.

CREDIT CARDS

Once you have proved to yourself and your parents that you can use a debit card responsibly, you may be ready for a credit card. If you are under eighteen, you will need a parent as a cosigner.

Working, Saving, and Spending Responsibly

LEGAL ISSUES FOR TEEN EMPLOYMENT

Before you accept a job, make sure what you are doing is legal. There are specific U.S. Department of Labor regulations regarding teen employment. The department's Web site for teens, Youth Rules (http://youthrules.dol.gov), offers a wealth of information for young workers. For example, fourteen- and fifteen-year-olds have strict limits on the total number of hours per day and per week that they can work. Federal laws allow employers to pay a youth minimum wage, which may be significantly less than the regular minimum wage. Workers at pools and amusement parks who are under sixteen have specific jobs that they are not allowed to do. For example, they cannot be slide monitors at the top of waterslides. Check the Youth Rules Web site to make sure that you are working at your job legally.

The U.S. Department of Labor's Youth Rules! Web site (http://www.youthrules.dol.gov) explains government regulations regarding teen employment.

This means your parent will be liable for your credit card debt if you can't pay.

A credit card differs from a debit card. A debit card acts like cash, so it is useful for everyday purchases such as clothing and food. A credit card is for larger items or emergencies. For example, your car may break down and need a tow and a repair. You may not have several hundred dollars in your checking account. However, using a credit card gives you some time to find the money to pay the bill.

It is very important to pay your credit card bill promptly. Many teens get credit cards with high interest rates. Paying off your credit card each month avoids costly finance charges and helps you build a good credit history.

TAXES

When you begin a paid job, you will fill out an Internal Revenue Service (IRS) form called a W-4. This form tells your employer how much money to withhold for taxes. Most workers pay federal and state income taxes, as well as Social Security and Medicare taxes. You won't have to pay any federal income taxes unless you make over a certain amount. In 2012, the amount was $7,600.

Some of the taxes withheld from your paycheck will be refunded when you file an income tax return. The basic tax form for individuals is called the 1040. You fill out this form to report your income for the year and figure out your tax obligations.

If you start your own business, and you make over a certain amount, you will have to pay self-employment income taxes. This is on your net profit. You can find this amount by subtracting any business expenses from your gross profit, or total profit. You will report all your income and expenses on an

Working, Saving, and Spending Responsibly

Filling out income tax forms is part of being a responsible worker.

IRS form called Schedule C Profit or Loss from Business, which you attach to the 1040 form. In addition, you will have to pay Social Security and Medicare taxes when self-employed. You can find information about these taxes on the IRS Web site at http://www.irs.gov.

Some teens work at jobs for which they earn unreported income. This is sometimes referred to as "working under the table." Workers mainly receive payment in cash. You might consider this attractive because you will not have taxes deducted from your paycheck. However, this is illegal. Your taxes are important contributions to a better life for everyone. They fund schools, health care, and parks. And your Social Security and Medicare taxes build security for your retirement.

Setting up bank accounts and paying taxes can be confusing. You may be tempted to let your parents or an accountant take care of your finances for you. However, figuring out your financial responsibilities can be empowering. You may make mistakes. But there are many resources available to help you. Take advantage of online tutorials and helpful phone numbers from your bank and the federal government. You will be making a huge investment in your future financial independence.

CHAPTER 6
This Is Just the Beginning: College Success and Career Building

Congratulations if you have discovered opportunities to earn money while working with kids. By working, you will save money for future needs. The experience you will gain is worth more than money, however. Your knowledge and skills can be used in new endeavors. Whether you volunteer or intern, work for others, or start your own business, you will see growth in your self-confidence, maturity, and motivation to succeed. How can you leverage your experiences into a promising future? Here are some suggestions.

UPDATE YOUR RÉSUMÉ

Any time you take a new job, internship, or volunteer position, you need to update your résumé. A résumé lists jobs and other work experience with the most recent first. If this is your first job, then it is especially important to write a powerful description. The following are some questions to think about when writing your résumé entry.

What exactly did you do in your position? To prepare to answer this, list all of your job duties from the time you arrive until the time you leave. A future employer will be able to see what you can do by what you have done.

What responsibilities did you have? For example, did you supervise a group of children? How many, and for what periods of time? Did you develop any original lessons, programs, or events? Did you work with any children with special needs? These kinds of details should be listed. They show that you are a trustworthy worker who can handle the responsibility of working with children.

Who will be able to verify your work? Your direct supervisor is a good person to add to your list of references. Ask your supervisor if it is all right for you to include him or her. Make sure you include all contact information for your references, such as phone numbers and e-mail addresses.

DISCOVER CAREER POSSIBILITIES

Has working with kids opened up this area as a possible career choice? If so, you might want to spend some time exploring career options working with children. There are incredible opportunities in the business, nonprofit, and educational communities. Reflecting on your experiences might help clarify your strengths and areas of interest. This will give you a head start in finding a rewarding career. The following are some career possibilities.

DAY CARE AND PRESCHOOLS

There will always be a need for workers at day care centers and preschools. While some education and training is needed, many of these positions do not require college degrees. Day care providers often work out of their own homes or in day care centers. Preschool teachers can work in independently owned, nonprofit, or nationally franchised schools. These schools often provide their own training. State teaching credentials are generally not required. Unlike elementary schools, many of these

This Is Just the Beginning: College Success and Career Building

CLASSES, CLUBS, AND MORE

You can start preparing now for a future working with children. Many high schools offer elective classes in child development. Some even run their own preschool or day care center. Some high schools have Future Teachers of America (FTA) clubs to encourage careers in education. All of these programs provide valuable training for students who want to explore careers with children.

Business classes are a good choice for teens who might want to become entrepreneurs in youth-oriented businesses. They teach students the fundamentals of small business, entrepreneurship, and economic theory. The Future Business Leaders of America has active chapters in many American high schools. They plan activities designed to promote self-confidence, leadership, and business skills. Junior Achievement (JA) is a nonprofit organization that teaches business skills to elementary, middle, and high school students. It offers classroom lessons and extracurricular activities that involve students in learning about workforce readiness, entrepreneurship, and financial literacy. Look for these organizations in your community.

schools follow a year-round schedule to accommodate working parents.

Teaching young children basic skills is fun and rewarding. The downside to these careers is that the pay is often lower than that of teachers with professional degrees.

CHILD-CENTERED ORGANIZATIONS

Many of the recreational facilities discussed earlier have potential career positions. These include managers or camp directors who hire, train, and supervise workers such as swimming teachers or camp counselors. They may help develop new programs, manage schedules and budgets, and deal with problems or concerns of children and families. Managers often learn on the job. They earn promotions by showing their supervisors that they can handle more responsibility. Though these positions have higher salaries, managers have less direct contact with children.

OWN A BUSINESS

An exciting possibility would be to develop your own business as an adult. Grow a part-time birthday party business into a thriving full-time career. Open a cooking school for young chefs or a coaching school for promising athletes. Art, music, and dance education can provide career opportunities for people with those talents. Although it is helpful, you do not necessarily need a college degree. Business and finance classes will provide useful information.

CAREERS THAT REQUIRE MORE EDUCATION

If you do decide to attend college, you may find that your experience working

This Is Just the Beginning: College Success and Career Building

with children can help you in many ways. First, you can use your experience as a topic for an application essay. Colleges are looking for students who can show that they have the maturity and motivation to be successful. In your essay you can describe your growth in leadership, responsibility, and problem-solving

A cooking school for young chefs would make a great small business.

Money-Making Opportunities for Teens Who Like Working with Kids

A variety of health professionals can have satisfying careers working with kids. Pediatricians are medical doctors who specialize in children's health.

This Is Just the Beginning: College Success and Career Building

ability. Discuss particular challenges that arose when working with children. Be specific in describing how you met those challenges.

Your time working with children might have helped you decide the type of work you want to do as a career. Some teens find they prefer a particular age group. Others are drawn to special needs children. They decide to pursue health careers or a career in special education.

Teens who commit to a bachelor's degree or higher will find opportunities in education, government, medicine, and nonprofits. In most states, K–12 public school teachers require a bachelor's degree and state certification. To earn these credentials, students take education classes and complete a certain number of hours of student teaching. They also take certification exams.

In addition to working in schools, teachers are sometimes employed at museums, zoos, and aquariums to coordinate activities for young visitors. Parks and visitors' centers often hire teachers, historians, or recreation specialists to design exhibits and plan activities for children.

Doctors, nurses, nutritionists, and other health professionals can specialize in working with children. Pediatricians and pediatric nurses are often in demand. Social workers, psychologists, and psychiatrists who treat children's mental health disorders can work in hospitals, clinics, or private practice.

You may have started working with kids because you thought it would be a fun way to spend a summer. Or maybe you thought expanding a popular babysitting business might have real money-making possibilities. Participating in the care and education of children can be full of challenges and adventure. It can provide opportunities for growing in maturity and gaining financially. No matter how you get started, working with children can become a rich and rewarding lifetime career.

GLOSSARY

AUTISM A serious disorder appearing in childhood that is characterized by an inability to relate to other people and severely limited use of language.

BIPOLAR DISORDER A major affective disorder that is characterized by episodes of mania and depression.

CEREBRAL PALSY A disorder marked by lack of muscle coordination, and sometimes speech defects, caused by brain damage present at birth or experienced during birth or infancy.

DOWN PAYMENT An initial payment made in cash at the time of purchase, with the balance to be paid later.

DOWN SYNDROME A condition caused by the presence of an extra copy of chromosome twenty-one, resulting in learning difficulties and physical differences, such as shorter stature.

FIXED COST An expense that does not change from time period to time period. It remains constant, even with an increase or decrease in the amount of goods or services produced.

GRATIFICATION A source of pleasure or enjoyment.

GROSS Total, as the amount of sales, salary, or profit before taking deductions for expenses or taxes.

INTEREST The charge for borrowing money or the return for lending it.

Money-Making Opportunities for Teens Who Like Working with Kids

INTERNAL REVENUE SERVICE (IRS) The U.S. government agency responsible for tax collection and tax law enforcement.

LUCRATIVE Producing money or wealth; profitable.

MANIPULATIVES Physical materials such as cubes, beads, and blocks that model mathematical concepts.

MEDICARE A national social insurance agency that provides health care for the elderly and disabled in the United States.

MINIMUM WAGE The lowest hourly wage employers are allowed to pay their employees according to federal law.

MUSCULAR DYSTROPHY A disease in which the muscles progressively waste away.

NET PROFIT The actual profit made on a business transaction after deducting all costs.

NONPROFIT An organization that is not intended to make a profit.

OVERDRAFT A deficit in a bank account caused by a person drawing more money than he or she had in the account.

RECONCILE To make sure one's accounts agree with bank statements.

SCHIZOPHRENIA A psychiatric disorder often characterized by hallucinations, delusions, and inappropriate reactions to situations.

Glossary

SOCIAL SECURITY A federal insurance program funded through payroll taxes to provide retirement and other benefits to those qualified to receive them.

SPINA BIFIDA A congenital condition that involves an imperfectly closed spinal column, often resulting in neurological disorders.

SPREADSHEET A financial worksheet in which data is organized into columns.

VARIABLE COST A cost that varies or changes from time to time so that it is unpredictable.

FOR MORE INFORMATION

American Camp Association (ACA)
5000 State Road 67 North
Martinsville, IN 46151-7902
(800) 428-2267
Web site: http://www.acacamps.org
The American Camp Association is a community of camp professionals who have joined together to share knowledge and experience and to ensure the quality of camp programs.

American Red Cross
2025 E Street NW
Washington, DC 20006
(202) 303-5214
Web site: http://www.redcross.org
The American Red Cross offers resources and classes in safety for babysitters, lifeguards, and swim instructors.

Future Business Leaders of America–Phi Beta Lambda, Inc.
1912 Association Drive
Reston, VA 20191-1591
(800) 325-2946
Web site: http://www.fbla-pbl.org
Future Business Leaders of America–Phi Beta Lambda is a nonprofit education association with a quarter million students preparing for careers in business and business-related fields.

Future Educators Association (FEA)
P.O. Box 7888
Bloomington, IN 47407-7888

For More Information

(800) 766-1156
Web site: http://www.futureeducators.org
The FEA is an organization for high school students who are interested in education careers. Its mission is to foster the recruitment and development of prospective educators worldwide.

International Volunteer Programs Association (IVPA)
P.O. Box 287049
New York, NY 10128
(646) 505-8209
Web site: http://www.volunteerinternational.org
The IVPA is an association of nongovernmental organizations involved in international volunteer work and internship exchanges. It can serve as a guide for those considering volunteering abroad or developing international service opportunities.

Junior Achievement USA
One Education Way
Colorado Springs, CO 80906
(719) 540-8000
Web site: http://ja.org
Junior Achievement is the world's largest organization dedicated to educating students about workforce readiness, entrepreneurship, and financial literacy through experiential, hands-on programs.

National AfterSchool Association (NAA)
8400 Westpark Drive, 2nd Floor
McLean, VA 22102
(703) 610-9002

Web site: http://www.naaweb.org
As the leading voice of the after-school profession, the NAA is dedicated to the development, education, and care of children and youth during their out-of-school hours.

Service Canada
Canada Enquiry Centre
Ottawa, ON K1A 0J9
Canada
(800) O-CANADA [622-6232]
Web site: http://www.servicecanada.gc.ca
Service Canada provides a wide range of career services and internship opportunities to Canadian citizens.

U.S. Department of Labor
Wage and Hour Division
Frances Perkins Building
200 Constitution Avenue NW
Washington, DC 20210
(866) 487-2365
Web site: http://www.dol.gov
The Department of Labor provides guidelines for student employment and internships and organizations that provide work and internship opportunities.

Youth Canada
140 Promenade du Portage, Phase IV, 4D392
Mail Drop 403
Gatineau, QC K1A 0J9
Canada

For More Information

Attn: Youth Operations Directorate
(800) 935-5555
Web site: http://www.youth.gc.ca
This one-stop resource center for Canadian youth offers information on education, employment, health, careers, and finance.

WEB SITES

Due to the changing nature of Internet links, Rosen Publishing has developed an online list of Web sites related to the subject of this book. This site is updated regularly. Please use this link to access the list:

http://www.rosenlinks.com/MMN/Kids

FOR FURTHER READING

Bailey, Diane. *Entrepreneurial Smarts* (Get Smart with Your Money). New York, NY: Rosen Publishing, 2013.

Baker, Jed. *No More Meltdowns: Positive Strategies for Managing and Preventing Out-of-Control Behavior.* Arlington, TX: Future Horizons, 2008.

Berger, Lauren. *All Work, No Pay: Finding an Internship, Building Your Résumé, Making Connections, and Gaining Job Experience.* Berkeley, CA: Ten Speed Press, 2012.

Bielagus, Peter G. *Quick Cash for Teens: Be Your Own Boss and Make Big Bucks.* New York, NY: Sterling, 2009.

Bochner, Arthur Berg, and Rose Bochner. *The New Totally Awesome Business Book for Kids: 20 Super Businesses You Can Start Right Now!* 3rd ed. New York, NY: Newmarket Press, 2007.

Bondy, Halley. *Don't Sit on the Baby: The Ultimate Guide to Sane, Skilled, and Safe Babysitting.* San Francisco, CA: Zest Books, 2012.

Bradshaw, Maddie. *Maddie Bradshaw's You Can Start a Business, Too!* Dallas, TX: M3 Girl Designs, 2010.

Canfield, Jack, Mark Victor Hansen, Heather McNamara, and Karen Simmons. *Chicken Soup for the Soul: Children with Special Needs: Stories of Love and Understanding for Those Who Care for Children with Disabilities.* Deerfield Beach, FL: Health Communications, 2007.

Fryer, Julie. *The Teen's Ultimate Guide to Making Money When You Can't Get a Job: 199 Ideas for Earning Cash on Your Own Terms.* Ocala, FL: Atlantic Publishing Group, 2012.

For Further Reading

Levine, Laura E., and Joyce Munsch. *Child Development: An Active Learning Approach*. Thousand Oaks, CA: SAGE Publications, 2011.

Mannix, Darlene. *Social Skills Activities for Special Children*. 2nd ed. San Francisco, CA: Jossey-Bass, 2009.

Mehlman, Barbara. *Babysitting Jobs: The Business of Babysitting* (Snap Books). Mankato, MN: Capstone Press, 2007.

Minden, Cecilia. *Starting Your Own Business* (21st Century Skills Library). Ann Arbor, MI: Cherry Lake Publishing, 2009.

Monteverde, Matthew. *Frequently Asked Questions about Budgeting and Money Management* (FAQ: Teen Life). New York, NY: Rosen Publishing, 2009.

Notbohm, Ellen. *Ten Things Every Child with Autism Wishes You Knew*. Rev. ed. Arlington, TX: Future Horizons, 2012.

Peters, Amy Jean. *How to Start a Home-Based Children's Birthday Party Business* (Home-Based Business Series). Guilford, CT: Globe Pequot Press, 2009.

Pitts, Pamela D. *Money 101: 14 Things Every Teen Should Know About Money*. Charleston, SC: Butterfly Financial, 2009.

Ragsdale, Susan, and Ann Saylor. *Great Group Games for Kids: 150 Meaningful Activities for Any Setting*. Minneapolis, MN: Search Institute Press, 2010.

Rankin, Kenrya. *Start It Up: The Complete Teen Business Guide to Turning Your Passions Into Pay*. San Francisco, CA: Zest Books, 2011.

Scheunemann, Pam. *Cool Jobs for Kids Who Like Kids: Ways to Make Money Working with Children* (Cool Kid Jobs). Edina, MN: ABDO Publishing Company, 2011.

Sember, Brette McWhorter. *The Everything Kids' Money Book: Earn It, Save It, and Watch It Grow!* 2nd ed. Avon, MA: Adams Media, 2010.

Toone, Matthew. *Great Games! 175 Games & Activities for Families, Groups, & Children*. Tulsa, OK: Müllerhaus Publishing Arts, 2009.

Toren, Adam, Matthew Toren, and Turonny Foo. *Kidpreneur$: Young Entrepreneurs with Big Ideas!* Phoenix, AZ: Business Plus Media Group, 2009.

Turner, Krista Thoren, and Entrepreneur Press. *Start Your Own Kid-Focused Business and More* (Entrepreneur Magazine's Startup). Irvine, CA: Entrepreneur Press, 2008.

Wittenberg, Renee. *Opportunities in Child Care Careers*. Rev. ed. New York, NY: McGraw-Hill, 2007.

BIBLIOGRAPHY

Business NH Magazine. "Teen Entrepreneur Toys with Success." April 2012, p. 10.

Capital One Financial Corporation. "News Release: Capital One's Annual Back-to-School Shopping Survey Reveals Gap in Budgeting Priorities and Communication Between Teens, Parents." August 5, 2010. Retrieved July 20, 2012 (http://phx.corporate-ir.net/phoenix.zhtml?c=70667&p=irol-newsArticle&ID=1456875&highlight).

CareerBuilder.com. "Thirty-Seven Percent of Companies Use Social Networks to Research Potential Job Candidates, According to New CareerBuilder Survey." April 18, 2012. Retrieved July 12, 2012 (http://www.careerbuilder.com/share/aboutus/pressreleasesdetail.aspx?id=pr691&sd=4%2F18%2F2012&ed=4%2F18%2F2099).

Centers for Disease Control and Prevention. "Disability and Health: Types of Disabilities." July 21, 2010. Retrieved July 16, 2012 (http://www.cdc.gov/ncbddd/disabilityandhealth/types.html).

Charles Schwab & Company. "2011 Teens & Money Survey Findings." Retrieved July 16, 2012 (http://www.aboutschwab.com/images/press/teensmoneyfactsheet.pdf).

CollegeBoard.org. "Trends in College Pricing 2011." Retrieved June 12, 2012 (http://trends.collegeboard.org/college_pricing).

ConsumerReports.org. "Don't Get Dinged by Overdraft Fees." Consumer Reports, June 2012. Retrieved October 1, 2012 (http://www.consumerreports.org/cro/magazine/2012/06/don-t-get-dinged-by-overdraft-fees/index.htm).

Cornell University Career Services. "Networking." 2012. Retrieved July 15, 2012 (http://www.career.cornell.edu/students/options/networking).

Delgado, Andrea. Interview with the author. Reno, NV, May 25, 2012.

Federal Interagency Forum on Child and Family Statistics. "America's Children in Brief: Key National Indicators of Well-Being, 2012." ChildStats.gov, 2012. Retrieved June 22, 2012 (http://www.childstats.gov/americaschildren/demo.asp).

Fogle, Angie. "Intern Blogger: Meet Fashion Closet Intern Angie Fogle." TeenVogue.com, June 16, 2010. Retrieved July 2, 2012 (http://www.teenvogue.com/teamvogue/blogs/intern/2010/06/meet-fashion-closet-intern-angie-fogle.html).

Gerber, Scott. "8 Kid Entrepreneurs to Watch." CNN Money, May 27, 2011. Retrieved July 18, 2012 (http://money.cnn.com/galleries/2011/smallbusiness/1105/gallery.kid_entrepreneurs/index.html).

IRS. "Understanding Taxes: The Quick and Simple Way to Understand Your Taxes." Retrieved June 20, 2012 (http://www.irs.gov/app/understandingTaxes/index.jsp).

Jump$tart Coalition for Personal Financial Literacy. "Making the Case for Financial Literacy—2011." Jumpstart.org, April 2011. Retrieved June 18, 2012 (http://www.jumpstart.org/assets/StateSites/LA/files/downloads/Making_the_Case_2011.pdf).

MarketingCharts.com. "Teen Tech Use Shapes Consumer Behavior." January 22, 2009. Retrieved July 16, 2012 (http://www.marketingcharts.com/interactive/teen-tech-use-shapes

Bibliography

-consumer-behavior-7638/experian-simmons-teens-spend-money-on-fall-2008jpg/).

Neal, Catherine. "Top Ten Places for Teens to Volunteer in San Jose, California." Yahoo! Voices, October 22, 2008. Retrieved June 10, 2012 (http://voices.yahoo.com/top-ten-places-teens-volunteer-san-jose-2072305.html?cat=25).

Petrecca, Laura. "Teen Entrepreneurs Offer Tips to Aspiring Peers." *USA Today*, May 19, 2009.

Ragsdell, Loretta A. "Young Coach Has Bright Future." *Austin Weekly News*, April 22, 2009. Retrieved May 30, 2012 (http://www.austinweeklynews.com/Main.asp?ArticleID=2220&SectionID=1&SubSectionID=1).

Scholastic News—Edition 4. "Dancin' on Wheels." December 7, 2009, p. 3.

Smithsonian National Zoological Park. "Teen Volunteers: Class Aide—National Zoo." Retrieved July 20, 2012 (http://nationalzoo.si.edu/Support/Volunteer/Teens/JuniorClassAide.cfm).

University of Texas M. D. Anderson Cancer Center. "Teen Volunteers—Available Teen Opportunities." 2012. Retrieved July 10, 2012 (http://www.mdanderson.org/how-you-can-help/volunteer/teen-volunteers/available-teen-opportunities/index.html).

USA Weekend. "Kids, Volunteering Is the 'Coolest Thing You Can Do.'" June 14, 2012, p. 8.

U.S. Department of Labor. "YouthRules! Preparing the 21st Century Workforce." 2012. Retrieved June 1, 2012 (http://www.youthrules.dol.gov).

U.S. Small Business Administration. "Teen Business Link." Retrieved June 20, 2012, (http://archive.sba.gov/teens/index.html).

Wood, Bev, and Rachel Wood. *I Can Earn It: The Make Money "How To" for Teens and Tweens*. Charleston, SC: Booksurge Publishing, 2009.

INDEX

A

accountants, 54
after-school programs, 9, 19
Alexander, Amiya, 30
Archer, Leanna, 47
autism, 14

B

babysitting, 6, 27, 28–29, 31, 35, 62
banking, 45, 48–50
before-school programs, 19
birthday party planning, 4, 6, 28, 29, 32, 58
blogs, 44
Boys & Girls Clubs of America, 20
brand, creating an original, 34
Bubble Ball, 27
budgets, 4, 32, 34, 58
business, owning a, 6, 9, 27–37, 44, 52–53, 55, 58
business plans, 31–35, 37

C

camp counselors, 21–22, 41, 57
certifications, 20, 29, 61
charities, 47–48
Chicago Chargers, 27

children, working with,
   career possibilities, 56–58
   education required, 58–62
   internships, 6, 38, 42–44, 55
   overview, 4–15
   tips, 9–13, 14–15
   traditional jobs, 16–26
   volunteering, 6, 38, 41–42, 55
Cieslewicz, Eric, 29–30
cover letters, 16, 23
CPR, 19
credit cards, 45, 50, 52

D

day care centers, 18, 19, 56, 57
debit cards, 45, 49, 50, 52
digital footprint, checking your, 17–18
disabilities, children with, 13–15, 41
Disney Channel, 42

E

emergency preparedness, 19, 20, 28, 35

F

Facebook, 17, 18
financial goals, setting, 45–48

77

first aid, 19, 28
fixed vs. variable costs, 31
Fogle, Angie, 44
Friends for Change, 42
Future Business Leaders of America (FBLA), 6, 57
Future Teachers of America (FTA), 57

G

Gonzalez, Asya, 47–48

I

Internal Revenue Service (IRS), 52, 53

J

Jessie, 42
job, finding a, 16–18
Junior Achievement (JA), 57

L

legal issues, and teen employment, 51
logo, creating a, 34

M

Medicare, 52, 53, 54
mentors, 42

minimum wage, 9, 51
money management, 4, 7, 9, 31, 32–34, 45–54

N

Nay, Robert, 27
networking, 17

P

playgroup, hosting a, 28, 29
power struggles, avoiding, 10–13
preschools, 18, 56, 57

R

Red Cross, 19, 20, 28
résumés, 16, 23, 42, 55–56
routine, establishing a, 10
Ryan, Debby, 42

S

She's Worth It!, 48
social media, 17–18, 44
Social Security, 52, 53, 54
social skills, teaching, 13

T

taxes, 45, 52–54
time management, 40

Index

tutoring, 6, 9, 20, 27, 31, 32
Twitter, 17, 18

U

U.S. Department of Labor, 45, 51
U.S. Small Business Administration (SBA), 27, 31, 32

W

Walker, Erin, 50
Willis, Michael, 27
Wood, Rachel, 37
word of mouth, 37
"working under the table," 53–54

Money-Making Opportunities for Teens Who Like Working with Kids

ABOUT THE AUTHOR

Susan Henneberg has been teaching high school and community college students in Reno, Nevada, to achieve their personal and academic goals for over thirty years. She enjoys reading, writing, and traveling. With her husband, Gene, she encourages her three daughters' adventures all over the world.

PHOTO CREDITS

Cover © iStockphoto.com/kali9; pp. 4–5, 8, 12, 40, 52–53 iStockphoto/Thinkstock; pp. 10–11 Stacy Gold/National Geographic Image Collection/Getty Images; p. 15 © Bill Aron/PhotoEdit; p. 17 Monkey Business Images/Shutterstock.com; p. 19 © Augusta Chronicle/ZUMA Press; pp. 20–21 © AP Images; p. 22 Jupiterimages/Creatas/Thinkstock; p. 25 Antoine Juliette/Oredia/Oredia Eurl/SuperStock; pp. 28–29 Kwame Zikomo/SuperStock; pp. 30–31 Andre J. Jackson/MCT/Landov; p. 33 Purestock/Getty Images; pp. 36–37, 39 Hemera/Thinkstock; p. 42–43 Jupiterimages/Polka Dot/Thinkstock; pp. 46–47 John Lund/Marc Romanelli/Blend Images/Getty Images; pp. 48–49 Blend Images/Ariel Skelley/the Agency Collection/Getty Images; p. 51 U.S. Department of Labor http://www.youthrules.dol.gov; pp. 58–59 © Anne Chadwick Williams/Sacramento Bee/ZUMA Press; pp. 60–61 CandyBox Images/Shutterstock.com; pp. 3, 4, 5, 63–80 (background image), page borders, boxed text backgrounds © iStockphoto.com/Tomasz Sowinski; back cover and remaining interior background image © iStockphoto.com/Pavel Khorenyan.

Designer: Brian Garvey; Editor: Andrea Sclarow Paskoff;
Photo Researcher: Karen Huang